A WINDY DAY

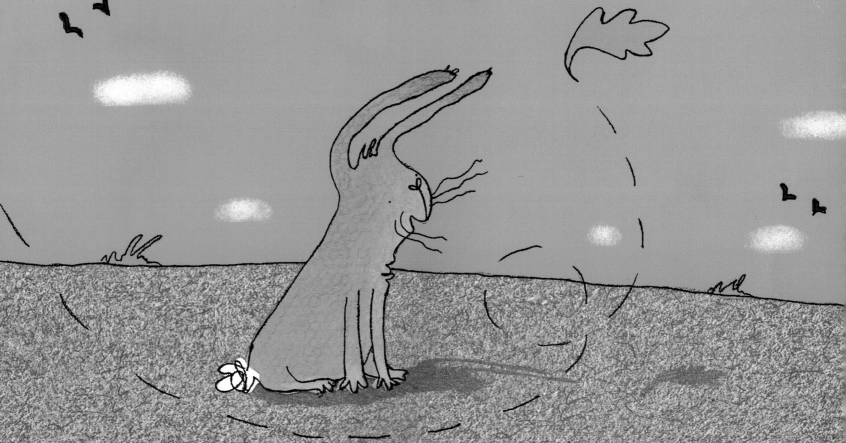

D0239124

With love to Emily and William

S.M.B.

for Carys, Cennydd and Steffan

C.M.

First published in Great Britain in 2007 by Gullane Children's Books
This paperback edition published in 2008 by

Gullane Children's Books

185 Fleet Street, London, EC4A 2HS
www.gullanebooks.com

1   3   5   7   9   10   8   6   4   2

Text copyright © Sheila M. Bird 2007
Illustrations copyright © Charlotte Middleton 2007

The right of Sheila M. Bird and Charlotte Middleton to be identified as the author and illustrator of this
work has been asserted by them in accordance with the Copyright, Designs and Patents Act, 1988.

A CIP record for this title is available from the British Library.

ISBN 978-1-86233-725-1

All rights reserved. No part of this publication may be reproduced, stored in a retrieval system,
or transmitted in any form or by any means, electronic, mechanical, photocopying,
recording or otherwise, without prior permission.

Printed and bound in Indonesia

A WINDY DAY

Sheila M. Bird

Illustrated by **Charlotte Middleton**

GULLANE
CHILDREN'S BOOKS

It was a windy day. The wind made whistle noises through the television aerials and seemed to send the birds flying backwards. William's mummy's hair whipped across her face and his sister Emily squealed as her skirt blew this way and that. William held on tight to the pushchair as they walked against the wind to nursery school.

It was so windy that William
decided to stay indoors at nursery and
paint a picture especially for his daddy.
William's daddy loved William's pictures.
They were hung on the walls of
his office, and the canteen . . .
and the cloakroom!

William stared at the blank sheet of paper wondering what to paint. His friend Adam had had no trouble deciding what to paint. He had painted himself . . . and the table, and the floor, and anyone unfortunate enough to pass him as he painted!

But William wanted his picture to be **extra special.**

A horse standing by a tree, in a field, with the sun shining.

William still hadn't painted his picture when it was time for
a story. All that was on the sheet of paper was his name and
a few stray splashes from Adam's painting. The story was about
a horse standing by a tree, in a field, with the sun shining.

Suddenly William knew what he wanted to paint. It would be . . .

a **horse**, standing by a **tree**,
in a **field**, with the **sun** shining.

As soon as he could, William got back to work.

He painted the
horse and the **tree trunk**
brown,

the **sun** bright
yellow

and he used the last of the
green paint on the **tree**,
so the field had to be
pink.

But it was a beautiful picture.
'A work of art,'
his teacher said.

William couldn't wait to show his picture to his
mummy and sister. It wasn't quite dry and the paint
on the horse's legs had run, making it look a lot taller
than it had when William painted it. But William's
mummy thought it was beautiful.
'Daddy will love that,'
she said as they left nursery school.

While walking home with the wind pushing them
on, Emily decided she rather liked the look of
William's painting. She wanted to hold it, but her
little hands were not as strong as William's and . . .

the fence and high into the sky.

Emily laughed at the pretty paper blowing in the wind. William's mummy gasped and William shouted 'Oh, no!'

Emily cried. William cried.
William's mummy felt like crying
as she tried to rescue the beautiful picture of

the **horse**, standing by a **tree**,
in a **field**, with the **sun** shining.

But it was
too high
and stuck fast in a tree,
so they all went home
feeling very, **very sad.**

A squirrel in the tree where the
picture had stuck took a good look at it.
'**My word,**' he said to himself, because
of course squirrels can't talk out loud.

'**What a beautiful picture of
a horse, standing by a tree,
in a field, with the sun shining.**'

As he thought this, the wind blew the picture from the tree into the air. It floated like a kite for a while before falling to the ground, right beside . . .

... a cow.

The cow looked at the picture. **'Goodness me,'** she said to herself, because of course cows can't talk out loud.

'What a beautiful picture of a **horse**, standing by a **tree**, in a **field**, with the **sun** shining.'

As she admired the picture, it was lifted by the wind which carried it like a leaf in autumn across the field to a . . .

. . . rabbit burrow.

A rabbit poked its head out of the burrow.
'**Well I never**,' said the rabbit to itself, because
of course rabbits can't talk out loud.

'What a beautiful picture of
a **horse**, standing by a **tree**,
in a **field**, with the **sun** shining.'

The rabbit called the rest of its family to see the
picture, but before they all had a chance to see it, the
wind had lifted it into the air and over a hedge to . . .

...the road!

The picture lay in the road for the rest of the afternoon.
A bicycle ran over it and left a tyre mark across the pink field.
A leaf stuck to it, making the horse look as if he were wearing a hat.

A car passed it . . . and stopped.
The driver got out to see what it was.

'What a splendid picture of
a **horse**, standing by a **tree**,
in a **field**, with the **sun** shining,'

he said to himself, because there was no one
else to hear him. 'I'll take it home with me.'

The driver of the car pulled up outside his house.
He searched in his pocket for his key.
He opened the front door.

And said to his family...

'Look at this fantastic picture of...

a **horse**,
standing by a **tree**,
in a **field**,
with the
sun shining.'

Everyone smiled.